PROJECT ROW HOUSES

**Where Everyone Is an Artist
and All People Sculpt Community:
Houston's Project Row Houses**

JULIE KNUTSON

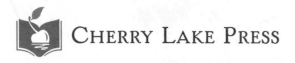

Published in the United States of America by Cherry Lake Publishing Group
Ann Arbor, Michigan
www.cherrylakepublishing.com

Reading Adviser: Marla Conn, MS, Ed., Literacy specialist, Read-Ability, Inc.
Photo Credits: © AMS Art Studios, cover, 1, 5, 13, 18, 20, 23, 26, 27, 28; © Everett Historical/Shutterstock.com, 9, 10; © Howard Chapman/Shutterstock.com, 14; © Cire notrevo/Shutterstock.com, 17

Cherry Lake Press is an imprint of Cherry Lake Publishing Group.

Library of Congress Cataloging-in-Publication Data
Names: Knutson, Julie, author.
Title: Project Row Houses / Julie Knutson.
Description: Ann Arbor, Michigan : Cherry Lake Publishing, [2021]. | Series: Changing spaces | Includes index. | Audience: Grades 4-6 | Summary: "Learn more about how Houston's Project Row Houses went from abandoned historic housing to vibrant art center and studio space. Explore the logistics of repurposing the land and buildings and meet the people who made it happen. The book showcases a range of 21st century skills—from "Flexibility & Adaptation" to "Creativity & Innovation"—and shows how moving away from a tear-down culture towards one of reuse helps tackle a host of critical challenges facing our planet and population. Thought-provoking questions and hands-on activities encourage the development of critical life skills and social emotional growth. Books in this series include table of contents, glossary of key words, index, author biography, sidebars, and infographics"—Provided by publisher.
Identifiers: LCCN 2020006421 (print) | LCCN 202006422 (ebook) | ISBN 9781534169043 (hardcover) | ISBN 9781534170728 (paperback) | ISBN 9781534172562 (pdf) | ISBN 9781534174405 (ebook)
Subjects: LCSH: Project Row Houses (Houston, Tex.)—Juvenile literature. | Artists and community—Texas—Houston—Juvenile literature. | Abandoned houses—Remodeling for other use—Texas—Houston—Juvenile literature.
Classification: LCC NX180.A77 K59 2021 (print) | LCC NX180.A77 (ebook) | DDC 700.1/03—dc23
LC record available at https://lccn.loc.gov/2020006421
LC ebook record available at https://lccn.loc.gov/2020006422

Cherry Lake Publishing Group would like to acknowledge the work of the Partnership for 21st Century Learning, a Network of Battelle for Kids. Please visit http://www.battelleforkids.org/networks/p21 for more information.

Printed in the United States of America
Corporate Graphics

With thanks to Eureka Gilkey of Project Row Houses

ABOUT THE AUTHOR

Julie Knutson is an author/educator fascinated by the endless ways in which people and communities can transform old spaces for new uses. She lives in Illinois with her husband, son, and extremely energetic border collie.

TABLE OF CONTENTS

Adaptive Reuse– More Than Meets the Eye

ESSENTIAL QUESTION: *How can entire communities participate in the creative transformation of neighborhoods and cities?*

Imagine for a moment what our world would be like if we approached everything around us as art and thought of everyone around us as artists. What if we viewed our communities as sculptures in which each resident wields the tools needed to mold and shape it? What if we regarded our neighborhoods, schools, towns, and cities as laboratories for creativity? What if we stopped thinking of art as something that belonged in museums and galleries and started thinking about it as something we produce

These homes are part of the unique Project Row Houses initiative. The spaces look to encourage neighborhood revitalization and resident empowerment.

every day, in every place? What if each and every one of us elevated the ordinary to the extraordinary?

At Project Row Houses (PRH) in Houston, Texas, people don't just preach these ideas; they practice them. Widely considered one of the largest **social sculptures** in the world, PRH is a community organization with a unique mission. As Executive Director Eureka Gilkey explains, that mission is to elevate "art as a tool to mobilize and enrich their community through **collective** action."

Social Sculpture

In the 1970s, artist Joseph Beuys (1921–1986) brought the notion of social sculpture to the forefront of the international art world. With a belief that all people are artists who can transform society for the better, Beuys conceived of collective, community arts actions. One of his best known was "7,000 Oaks" (1982). With this action, Beuys led an effort to reforest parts of his native Germany with 7,000 trees, particularly in areas that bore the scars of World War II.

Across the world, countless others have embraced the idea. In Culiacán, Mexico, for example, artist Pedro Reyes collected 1,527 weapons, which he melted down and re-formed into shovels in his action "Palas por Pistolas." This showed how an "agent of death" could be transformed into an "agent of life." These shovels were used to plant 1,527 trees. From Vancouver to Paris to Denver, those same shovels have been used by schoolchildren and museum organizations for planting the same number of trees.

The spark for PRH came from a group of artists known as the Magnificent Seven in the early 1990s. They had their eye on a cluster of 22 vacant and broken-down **shotgun-style** houses built by early African American settlers in Houston. The city wanted to tear down these long-unattended former residences. But the artists' collective saw in these houses the promise of preserving the community's history. They also saw in them the promise of creating a place where people could gather to talk about everyday issues and challenges—and try to solve them creatively.

This is the story of how these 22 run-down houses were **adaptively reused** as an arts hub, giving new life not just to a series of structures, but also to Houston's Third Ward community.

CHAPTER 1

The Third Ward: A Historic Hub of African American Life in Houston

After the Civil War, Houston's Third Ward grew into a vibrant center of African American culture, business, and social life. Drawn by the promise of urban opportunity, formerly enslaved people from the counties surrounding Houston moved into the city. This continued well into the 20th century. Between 1910 and 1930, the neighborhood's African American population swelled from 22,929 to 66,357.

The American Civil War ended in 1865. Many African Americans fought to help end slavery.

Segregation and discrimination was widespread across the United States—and especially in the South—for much of the 20th century.

The city was segregated under **Jim Crow laws**, so the Third Ward developed its own self-sustaining ecosystem. Leaders like Reverend John Henry "Jack" Yates led efforts to pool community resources to buy land for a public park. Emancipation Park was created in 1872. It provided one of the few public spaces open to African Americans in the entire state, serving as an important gathering site for annual Juneteenth celebrations.

Juneteenth: A Day to Celebrate Freedom

President Abraham Lincoln signed the Emancipation Proclamation on January 1, 1863, legally freeing America's enslaved population. However, news of the document didn't reach Texas until June 19, 1865. Today, Texans continue to celebrate "Juneteenth" in commemoration of this historic announcement.

Elsewhere in the neighborhood, performance venues like the Eldorado Ballroom welcomed internationally known artists such as B. B. King and Ray Charles. By 1950, more than 150 black-owned businesses lined the Third Ward's main avenue. At one point in its history, the Ward boasted over 90 churches. More than places for worship, churches also served as civic centers, where social activism during the civil rights movement took off. It is this history that PRH celebrates and builds upon.

Desegregating Houston

Students from the Third Ward's Texas Southern University (TSU) played a major role in desegregating the city's institutions. On March 4, 1960, TSU students staged a sit-in at the counter of Weingarten's grocery store at 4110 Alameda Street. While they were served only insults and abuses, they inspired city leaders to take action to quickly and peacefully desegregate Houston businesses.

PRH builds upon the Third Ward's legacy of community involvement and activism.

These wooden, shotgun-style homes were easily built with limited resources.

In its early years of settlement in the 1880s and 1890s, more than 25 percent of African American residents of the Ward owned their homes. The most common building type was the shotgun house, so named because it was said you could shoot a shotgun straight through, from the front to the back door. This **vernacular** style can be traced from Africa to the Caribbean to New Orleans.

From there, the style spread throughout the United States. Its significance in the African American architectural tradition has been upheld by artists including John Biggers, who influenced the thoughts and practices of the Magnificent Seven. To Rick Lowe, another founding member, reusing these structures that embodied the **ingenuity** of former Ward residents seemed like a way to move toward the future while preserving the community's historic past.

CHAPTER 2

Out of the Studio, into the Community: Making Social Sculpture

When artist Rick Lowe first caught sight of the 22 shotgun houses in the early 1990s, they were in a state of major disrepair. From the 1960s onward, the Third Ward suffered an exit of residents and businesses. After Houston desegregated, new parts of the city opened up to African Americans. As a result, many upper-income black families left the Third Ward. The neighborhood's population declined, and many homes were left vacant. In 1992, Lowe toured the Third Ward with community organizers, city officials, and developers. The group was told that this city block at Oak and Holman Streets was the "worst" in the whole neighborhood. Each of the row houses that stood on it was destined to be torn down.

[21ST CENTURY SKILLS LIBRARY]

Vacant homes can pose safety and social risks. Many of those homes in the Third Ward were set to be torn down.

After the tour, Lowe shared this information with his fellow Magnificent Seven artists, who also wanted to support and preserve the historic Third Ward. He reminded them of John Biggers's paintings, which celebrated the role of these structures as a material link between people of African descent across continents. Lowe had also been adapting his own art, moving more and more out of the studio and into the community. This was partially inspired by the idea of "social sculpture" advanced by Joseph Beuys—and partially by a challenge issued by a high schooler on a class visit to his studio.

PRH is a large-scale art installation that serves
and is shaped by its community.

As Lowe remembers, the student "told me that, sure, the work reflected what was going on in his community, but it wasn't what the community needed . . . If I was an artist, he said, why didn't I just come up with some kind of creative solution to issues, instead of just telling people like him what they already knew."

For Lowe and his fellow socially conscious artists, the row houses that city officials largely viewed as a **blight** provided an opportunity. That opportunity was to harness the power of collective action to create arts-based solutions in conversation with the community.

The Magnificent Seven

Artists often work in groups called collectives as a means of exchanging ideas and supporting creative development. The Magnificent Seven is a group of—you guessed it—seven artists who teamed up to create new opportunities for the arts and "new models for living creatively, gracefully, politically." They are James Bettison, Bert Long Jr., Jesse Lott, Rick Lowe, Floyd Newsum, Bert Samples, and George Smith.

Locally created and curated art exhibits rotate through PRH.

After purchasing the block and a half of properties in 1993, the artists' organization began renovating each of the 538-square-foot (50-square-meter) houses. The process drew not just the core group of artists, but also community members and volunteers of all ages. Area arts organizations—notably, the Menil Foundation and DiverseWorks—also banded together to support the transformation.

Continued Support for Creative Growth

Two famous Houstonians—Grammy Award winners Beyoncé and Solange Knowles—stay connected to the Third Ward neighborhood where they grew up. When Solange received the Lena Horne Prize for Artists Creating Social Impact, she donated the $100,000 award to PRH.

One by one, the houses were restored. Rotting boards were replaced. **Facades** were brightened. Trees and shrubs were replanted. The interiors were primed for showcasing art, nurturing community dialogue, and providing education and social services to Third Ward residents.

It was the dawn of a new day for both the 22 houses and for each and every person who walked through their doors.

CHAPTER 3

A Living, Community Sculpture

For nearly 3 decades, Project Row Houses has evolved and adapted to meet changing neighborhood needs. Its initial 22 houses have grown to 39 structures. Today, these buildings host not just art installations and performances, but also after-school tutoring programs, markets for local makers and food producers, business development offices, programs for young mothers, and affordable housing. Each program is rooted in the idea of social sculpture: we are all artists who possess the power to transform our own lives and communities. To do so, we need to identify our vision for ourselves and develop creative ways to reach that vision.

The Healthy Women Houston project encourages visitors to "receive and share resources and stories to improve the health of black women and their community."

Reviving and Living a Dream

What does living creatively every day look like? Look no further than Third Ward resident Eugene Howard. After being **incarcerated** for more than 20 years, Eugene returned to the neighborhood. He struggled to figure out how and where he fit in after 2 decades in prison. PRH staff encouraged him to explore and identify his passions. When Rick Lowe learned that Eugene loved to cook and wished he owned a restaurant, he made up a poster that profiled Eugene as a superstar chef. The poster caught on, spawning aprons, T-shirts, and mugs bearing Eugene's likeness. Out of this, he started a pop-up restaurant, becoming both a community leader and realizing his dream.

At PRH, art exhibits and events are shaped around themes of political, social, environmental, and economic importance. These themes range from disaster relief responses to Black Lives Matter to health care. The community can view the artwork created on these themes and also attend workshops, talks, and **symposia** on them. Youth artists have worked in teams on projects ranging from designing and building an art car for Houston's annual Art Car Parade to creating and stitching patches for a quilt someday destined for space.

Intergalactic Art

NASA's Lyndon B. Johnson Space Center is located just 25 miles (40 kilometers) southeast of PRH. In 2007 and 2008, astronaut Leland Melvin visited with children in the PRH education program. He invited them to make a piece of art that he could bring on his next trip to space. Inspired by artist Faith Ringgold, the children crafted a quilt that showed views of the Third Ward and beyond from space.

New members of the PRH family are inducted every year.

Within the walls of PRH's historic structures, efforts to preserve community identity and fight off **gentrification** also take shape. Big issues—such as developing affordable housing with a low-environmental footprint—are explored with community partners from Rice University's architecture school. Business incubators offer **entrepreneurs** start-up funds to bring their

Businesses like the Progressive Amateur Boxing Association
support the PRH community and its members.

The PRH social sculpture is always evolving.

ideas to reality. And for decades, the Young Mothers Residential Program has provided affordable housing and a creative, nurturing environment for new moms and their children.

Built out of houses that once sheltered emancipated people and reshaped, molded, and adapted into a home for an entire community, PRH is, and will continue to be, a place for preserving history and pursuing dreams.

Extend Your Learning

PRH encourages residents to participate in documenting the history and changing nature of the Third Ward. Select a historic building in your community and research the following questions:

- Who built it?

- When and why was it constructed? What materials and resources were used?

- How has it been used throughout time? Have its uses changed?

Ask your local librarian to help you locate old photos or newspaper accounts of the structure.

Then, turn your camera's lens on this building to show what it looks like today. Ask parents, grandparents, neighbors, and friends how the structure has changed in their lifetimes. Record their responses.

Share your findings through a short documentary video that highlights the changing nature of this place across time.

Glossary

adaptively reused (uh-DAP-tiv-lee ree-YOOZD) to reuse a structure for a purpose other than that which it was originally designed to serve

blight (BLITE) visible decline or decay

collective (kuh-LEK-tiv) as a group

entrepreneurs (ahn-truh-pruh-NURZ) people who launch, organize, and operate a business

facades (fuh-SAHDZ) the front parts of buildings that face the street

gentrification (jen-trih-fuh-KAY-shuhn) when spaces in a community are renovated and rebuilt, and housing becomes too expensive for its longtime residents

incarcerated (in-KAR-suh-ray-tid) imprisoned or in jail

ingenuity (in-juh-NOO-ih-tee) inventiveness

Jim Crow laws (JIM KROH LAWZ) laws in the United States that legalized segregation from the late-19th to mid-20th centuries and set different rules for black and white Americans

shotgun-style (SHAHT-guhn STILE) a one-story, one-room-wide house

social sculptures (SOH-shuhl SKUHLP-churz) ideas advocated by artist Joseph Beuys that art can transform society if all actions are thought of creatively and if all citizens are regarded as creators

symposia (sim-POH-zee-uh) conferences or meetings developed around a set topic

vernacular (vur-NAH-kyuh-lur) architecture that is found in a specific place, built with specific materials

INDEX